State of Fire

D.S.Pais

Ukiyoto Publishing

All global publishing rights are held by

Ukiyoto Publishing

Published in 2023

Content Copyright © D.S.Pais

ISBN 9789359207704

*All rights reserved.
No part of this publication may be reproduced,
transmitted, or stored in a retrieval system, in any
form by any means, electronic, mechanical,
photocopying, recording or otherwise, without the
prior permission of the publisher.*

The moral rights of the authors have been asserted.

*This is a work of fiction. Names, characters,
businesses, places, events, locales, and incidents are
either the products of the author's imagination or
used in a fictitious manner. Any resemblance to
actual persons, living or dead, or actual events is
purely coincidental.*

*This book is sold subject to the condition that it shall
not by way of trade or otherwise, be lent, resold,
hired out or otherwise circulated, without the
publisher's prior consent, in any form of binding or
cover other than that in which it is published.*

www.ukiyoto.com

Dedication

To my family, whose unwavering support and love have been my guiding light throughout this journey. Your encouragement and belief in me have been the foundation upon which this book was built.

Acknowledgments

I would like to express my heartfelt gratitude to all those who contributed to the creation of this book.

I would like to acknowledge the publishing team, whose expertise and creativity transformed the manuscript into a polished book. Your attention to detail and commitment to quality are truly commendable.

Last but not least, I am grateful to my friends and colleagues who provided encouragement, feedback, and a supportive network throughout this process.

To all of you who played a part, whether big or small, in bringing this book to life, thank you. Your contributions have made this journey not only possible but immensely rewarding.

Contents

Chapter 1	1
Chapter 2	5
Chapter 3	10
Chapter 4	14
Chapter 5	18
Chapter 6	23
Chapter 7	28
Chapter 8	33
Chapter 9	38
Chapter 10	41
Chapter 11	44
About the Author	46

Chapter 1

In the dimly lit room, an eerie silence hung in the air, broken only by the soft rustle of paper. The scene was haunting, with a pile of handwritten letters meticulously stacked on a table as if they held the weight of a soul's deepest turmoil. These letters, a poignant testament to the internal struggles of a tormented individual, whispered tales of despair, longing, and an unquenchable thirst for love.

It was a mystery that gripped the minds of those who encountered this somber tableau. Each neatly arranged letter seemed to be a piece of the intricate puzzle that was Gianna's life. The collective story they told was one of a person teetering on the precipice of desperation, yearning for a love that may have been unrequited.

The contents of these letters were a revelation, a glimpse into the depths of Gianna's heart. One note unveiled a shocking truth—Gianna had allegedly made a harrowing attempt on her own life. Her physical ailment mirrored the emotional turmoil that had consumed her existence. But there was more, a clandestine layer of her pain that remained hidden, waiting to be uncovered.

Issac, a central figure in Gianna's life, stood unknowingly at the crossroads of her emotions. Little did he realize that Gianna had poured her heart onto paper, etching her uncertainties about his affection. A poignant declaration adorned one letter, proclaiming, "This will be the best way out, as I cannot bear to see another girl have him." The words were etched in ink, an undeniable testament to her inner turmoil.

A handwriting expert lent their expertise to the unfolding narrative, confirming what the heart-wrenching letters suggested—Gianna's soul had indeed found its expression in those written words. The inked script carried the weight of her pain, etched onto paper as if her thoughts had found solace in this tangible form.

The revelations cascaded further, revealing a twisted thread in the tale. The letters unveiled Gianna's attempt on both her life and Issac's, a chilling realization that cast a new light on her struggle. Issac, miraculously, emerged from this ordeal, a survivor of the darkness that had claimed Gianna. Her story took on a tragic hue as the realization sunk in—she hadn't been as fortunate.

The pages continued to unfold the inner workings of Gianna's heart, her words painting a vivid picture of her unwavering affection for Issac. "When you love someone, you love him," she had written, her emotions laid bare on the paper. In her vulnerability, she acknowledged that her hopes of finding true love had been dashed, realizing that her place in Issac's heart was but a fleeting moment in time.

The final chapter of this poignant saga was a letter addressed to Mrs. Lukas, a poignant testament to Gianna's final moments. Penned just a day before her passing, this missive held an air of finality, a whisper of impending closure. Gianna's words painted a vivid scene, describing the presence of Jerrie, a tangible connection to her past. "Jerrie is in the boat outside somewhere," she wrote, alluding to an imminent departure from the realm of the living. Her words held an eerie tranquillity, a resignation to the fate she had chosen.

As the letter requested, Jerrie was entrusted with this final piece of Gianna's legacy, a solemn duty to ensure its delivery. The words seemed to carry a weight beyond the ink and paper, a message of closure and release.

The tale of Gianna's life, as revealed through these meticulously penned letters, was one of heartache, longing, and a desperate search for a love that ultimately eluded her. Each word etched on paper was a glimpse into her soul, a raw and unfiltered expression of her innermost thoughts.

In the dimly lit room, where the letters lay stacked with purposeful precision, Gianna's voice echoed.

Chapter 2

In the heart of their love story, Gianna and John found themselves deeply enamored, with dreams of a blissful life together.

Gianna, a vibrant 21-year-old bank worker, and John, known as Issac, had a connection that spanned years, fostering a bond that eventually culminated in the desire for marriage. Hailing from Mimico, Ontario, Canada, Gianna was a capable employee at the bank, admired for her dedication and skills. Her life was interwoven with Issac's, their love story becoming a beacon of hope for a future steeped in happiness.

Yet, obstacles loomed on their path to marital bliss. Gianna's father, a Polish immigrant, held reservations about their marriage due to religious differences, as Issac was not a Roman Catholic. In a bid to quell these concerns, Issac, aged 26, chose to convert to Catholicism, a symbolic gesture that demonstrated his commitment to Gianna and their shared future. Despite this monumental step, the families remained unconvinced, driving Gianna and Issac to contemplate drastic measures. Gianna's family didn't have an issue with Issac but were worried about his best man. Gianna's sister, Celine, thought Jerrie was in love with Gianna.

Amidst opposition and familial discord, the young couple made the heart-wrenching decision to embark on a secret marriage. Their love was unwavering, and they chose to cement their commitment in the face of adversity. A clandestine ceremony was planned, devoid of family presence, the weight of their decision adding to the gravity of their love story.

As the chosen day arrived, Gianna and Issac found themselves on the precipice of a new chapter. In the eleventh hour, however, unexpected visitors arrived, shrouding the occasion in uncertainty. Gianna's sisters, motivated by concern, pleaded with her to reconsider. An emotional tug-of-war ensued, escalating to a point where the authorities were summoned by alarmed neighbors. The sisters eventually departed, leaving behind a complex tapestry of emotions.

Amidst the turmoil, an underlying concern arose—a worry not directed at Issac, but rather at his best man, Jerrie. Gianna's sister, Celine, held suspicions that Jerrie's affections might extend beyond the boundaries of friendship. Her intuition introduced a new layer of complexity to the unfolding of

Gianna's love story, hinting at hidden dynamics beneath the surface.

The date was etched in history—May 12th, 1947—marking the day when Gianna and Issac eloped, sealing their bond in a union that transcended societal conventions. Issac, a war veteran serving in the dental corps, was a man of resilience and strength, a testament to the challenges he had faced and overcome. His steadfast companion, Jerrie, stood by his side. An Italian immigrant and a professional ballroom dancer, Jerrie shared a deep bond with Issac, forged over years of camaraderie.

The trio—Issac, Gianna, and Jerrie—formed an inseparable unit, sharing their lives and moments. While the closeness was evident, the peculiarity of Jerrie accompanying the newlyweds on their honeymoon raised eyebrows. The unusual circumstance prompted questions, with the dynamics of their relationship coming under scrutiny.

Gianna's feelings for Issac remained steadfast, her love an unwavering constant in her life. She viewed Jerrie not as a rival, but as a confidant of Issac's, someone whose presence was comforting rather than unsettling. Maybe she stood as the embodiment of the idea that love truly knows no boundaries. Amidst their voyage, Gianna's introspections mirrored a sense of comprehension. She pondered whether Jerrie's motives were fuelled by a wish to steadfastly bolster Issac, his closest companion, precisely when such support was most crucial.

Following their secret nuptials, the newlyweds, now christened the Campbells, embarked on their initial days of wedded life. A rented apartment in Toronto became their sanctuary, their love radiating within the confines of their shared space. It was during this period that Jerrie continued to be a part of their lives, a presence that, while unorthodox, seemed to carry a sense of familiarity.

Their journey took a turn as they ventured to Jerrie's cottage in Celestial Falls on May 17th, 1947. Nestled amidst the tranquillity of nature, the cottage stood as a remote haven accessible only by boat. A surprising twist awaited ----Jerrie accompanied the couple throughout their honeymoon.

As the days unfolded in the rustic solitude of Celestial Falls, a disconcerting change came over Gianna. Emotional fluctuations became evident, with episodes of crying bouts and a sense of detachment from reality. Within this backdrop, Gianna found herself drawn into conversations with Jerrie, discussions that centered around the core of her anxieties—Issac's love for her. These heart-to-heart exchanges unearthed a layer of vulnerability, revealing Gianna's deep-seated insecurities.

Chapter 3

Gianna was in a serene, rustic setting—a secluded cabin tucked away in Celestial Falls. But beneath the tranquil exterior, a storm of emotions was brewing, a tale of love, and doubt.

She was gripped by an inexplicable moodiness, punctuated by moments of disorientation that left her seemingly unresponsive. An aura of doubt hung over her, leading her to seek solace in drugs to escape her troubles. In her vulnerable state, she turned to Jerrie, seeking answers to the doubts that gnawed at her heart.

"Does Issac truly love me?" The uncertainty that had silently simmered within her demanded answers, and Jerrie became the unwitting confidant of her innermost fears.

Gianna had finished cooking and she had made hot chocolate and porridge. She was gazing out the window, at which point she asked Jerrie for a pen to write a letter to Mrs. Lukas.

Days turned into a muddled haze, and May 20th marked a pivotal moment in their fateful narrative. On that day, Jerrie left the cabin, leaving Gianna and Issac behind as he ventured out for some sunbathing.

Returning to his cabin later that evening, Jerrie was met with a horrifying sight—the cabin was engulfed in flames, an inferno that devoured their sanctuary. Panic and chaos took over as he rushed to find his friends. Amidst the flames, he discovered Issac, wounded and disoriented, bleeding from a head injury. In an act of courage, Jerrie dragged Issac from the fire's grasp, struggling against the raging elements to save his friend.

But amid the chaos and the consuming flames, Gianna was missing. Desperation seized Jerrie as he searched, crying out for help from the neighborhood that had rushed to the scene. The fire raged on, relentless and unforgiving, consuming the cabin and all it held within.

As the hours wore on, the cabin succumbed to the blaze's fury, reducing their abode to smoldering ruins. Yet, amid the devastation, Jerrie's thoughts were consumed by the well-being of his friends. Determined, he ferried Issac to safety, rushing him to the hospital to ensure his recovery.

It was in the hospital's confines that Jerrie's course of action took a new turn. With Issac's safety secured, he reached out to the authorities, contacting the police to unravel the events that had led to the catastrophe. Questions lingered in the air, and the truth seemed to elude them, shrouded in the smoke and ash of the consumed cabin.

But as darkness descended that fateful night, a neighbor stumbled upon a chilling discovery—a lifeless body, lying amidst shallow water. The proximity of this gruesome find to the site of the fire sent shivers down spines. It was Gianna, clad in her floral pajamas, her life tragically extinguished. She lay face down, a stark image in contrast to the serene surroundings.

The discovery painted a grim picture, and confusion reigned. How had she ended up there? Why had she not escaped the raging flames? As the elements gradually intertwined, a disconcerting storyline began to surface. Despite the fire's destructive might, Gianna's body was devoid of any burns or signs of violence, leaving investigators perplexed.

An autopsy would reveal a clue—traces of codeine were found in her stomach, hinting at a substance that had played a role in her final moments. And yet, it was not the codeine that claimed her life.

Gianna's cause of death was declared as drowning. The river had claimed her, a stark contrast to the fiery inferno that had consumed their cabin.

Intriguingly, a first responder to the fire contradicted this narrative. Major Daniel Gutierrez, who had been on the scene to battle the flames, reported not having seen Gianna's lifeless form earlier when he had been seeking water to douse the blaze. The mystery deepened, and the pieces of the puzzle seemed to blur into an enigmatic whole.

Issac had a ring that had been borrowed from a married friend—a ring that had held the promise of a proposal to Gianna. But this ring, like the lives it touched, vanished into the shadows, leaving behind a legacy marked by questions, uncertainty, and a profound sense of loss.

In this intricate tapestry of love, doubt, and tragedy, there was a haunting allure of unanswered questions.

Chapter 4

It seemed like a small town gripped by intrigue, where the lines between reality and speculation blurred in the shadows of a mysterious tragedy. The perplexing demise of Gianna seemed like a story that defied easy explanation. Her tale seemed to have unbelievable twists and turns, marked by questions, suspicions, and a quest for truth. The tragedy was attributed by Gianna's family to the two men, as they suspected foul play and arrived at a definitive conclusion.

Gianna's farewell had taken place on May 26th, a somber reminder of a life cut short. The very church that bore witness to her wedding just two weeks prior stood as a backdrop to her final journey. Emotions swirled as the community gathered, a mosaic of grief and curiosity marking the occasion.

Issac, Jerrie, and a cast of others then find themselves thrust into the spotlight of a police investigation. The case unravels like a tangle of threads, each person's role a puzzle piece in the larger picture. Issac, once released from the hospital, becomes the focal point of scrutiny. Burns, shock, a head injury, and a clouded memory are the remnants of his ordeal.

Meanwhile, Jerrie, an integral player in this tale, undergoes a marathon interrogation that stretches over 13 grueling hours. His account, a verbose 3,000-word narrative, leaves the police baffled. Described as "fantastic," the police's skepticism echoes through the corridors of the investigation. The absurdity of the situation seems to cast doubt on the authenticity of his statement, his words bordering on the realm of the improbable.

Jerrie, known in some circles as Jerrie Ciufo, emerges as a character marked by complexity. A man who journeyed from Italy to Canada in pursuit of success, he found his footing elusive in the construction and insurance domains.

The courtroom doors swing open, revealing a dramatic inquest that ignites curiosity and intrigue. It was June 19th, already a month had passed by after the tragedy had taken place and the town of Bracebridge, Ontario was drawn to the unfolding spectacle. Crowds gathered spectators began jostling for a view, lining up outside, even seeking autographs from the very men at the heart of this labyrinthine saga. Media frenzy adds fuel to the fire, with sensational coverage splashed across the pages of the Toronto Daily Star.

As the days unfold within the courtroom, revelations surface like ripples on a pond. Jerrie's marathon questioning leaves a trail of questions, his level of involvement in the couple's life raising eyebrows. His vehement denial of seeking to join the honeymoon, attributing his presence to mere convenience, is met with skeptical eyes. The very idea that he orchestrated the couple's secret marriage is deemed ludicrous, yet the tendrils of suspicion weave their way into the investigation.

Issac, a survivor bearing physical and emotional scars, steps into the limelight of interrogation. Three hours of questioning yield an unsettling result—his memory fades beyond breakfast with Jerrie and Gianna on the day of the incident. A fog descends, obscuring the events that followed, leaving investigators grasping at shadows.

In the courthouse in Bracebridge, interest is piqued, lines form and the atmosphere buzzes with anticipation. The narrative of the case becomes a part of the town's fabric, seeping into the conversations, and becoming a fixture in tabloids and newspapers across Toronto.

In the tangled web of the case, signs emerge that paint a sinister picture. The absence of burns or physical marks on Gianna's body challenges the narrative of her accidental death. She is found barefoot by the river's edge, a stark contrast to the tumultuous blaze that engulfed their cabin. Traces of codeine in her stomach add complexity to the puzzle.

A neighbor's account offers a peculiar contradiction—the exact spot where Gianna's lifeless form was discovered had been traversed by the neighbor earlier, seeking water to extinguish the flames. The timeline bends, and questions arise—had Gianna's body been placed after the fire's fury had abated? Despite the contradictions, the ultimate cause of her death is ruled as drowning.

Truth often lies veiled beneath layers of ambiguity.

In the same mannerisms as that of Gianna's family, the police have their suspicions about how close Jerrie was to the couple. Jerrie was vehement that he did not even want to accompany the couple on their honeymoon but had done so out of the convenience of driving them to his cabin. The police even theorized that Jerrie had somehow arranged the marriage which to Jerrie was absurd.

Chapter 5

In the aftermath of Gianna's passing, the possibility of suicide lingered like a haunting specter. The letters she penned in the months leading up to her demise cast a shadow of doubt over the circumstances surrounding her death, painting a portrait of a tormented soul caught in the throes of despair. These letters, presented later in the trial, held the power to shift the course of the investigation, steering it towards the unsettling realm of self-inflicted tragedy.

Gianna's life revealed a series of notes that lay bare her innermost thoughts. Written in moments of darkness, these letters provided a glimpse into the turmoil that plagued her. Alarming in their content, they formed the basis of the suicide theory that would hang over the investigation. The letters were, often, addressed to Jerrie, a central figure in Gianna's life, and the man who seemed to hold a unique place in her heart.

She begins writing these letters on April 6th, Easter Sunday—a day of celebration and reflection. Gianna's words paint a somber image of disappointment, a poignant expression of her longing for Issac's proposal. Issac's recollection of the day is hazy; he remembers Gianna being unwell, but he remained oblivious to her hidden struggles and the letter addressed to Jerrie.

As April unfolded, Gianna's despair seemed to deepen, finding its outlet in the written word. Another letter emerged this time a heart-wrenching testament to her inner pain. She expressed her desire not only for her demise but to take Issac with her. The words carried a raw emotion, the agony of unrequited love etched onto paper.

The complexity of her emotions was further laid bare in a subsequent letter, her thoughts spinning a web of yearning and resignation. The stark realization that her place in Issac's heart was transient added to the weight of her emotional struggles.

The climax of this tragic saga rested in a letter penned the day before her death. A missive addressed to the owner of the cabin, it alludes to Jerrie's presence on the boat, a cryptic message that hints at impending finality. The letter's words have a haunting quality, a foreshadowing that leaves a chill in the air.

Jerrie's role becomes increasingly complex, as he emerges as the custodian of these letters, saving them from the flames that engulfed their cabin. The act of preservation seems to speak volumes, an eerie testament to the veracity of Gianna's emotional turmoil. Jerrie successfully rescued the documents but couldn't save Gianna.

The silence Jerrie weighs heavy—his knowledge of Gianna's suicidal tendencies remained veiled from Issac until the inquiry. This revelation evoked a mix of emotions, from empathy to suspicion. Issac's forgiveness for Jerrie's silence stems from a belief that his friend was motivated by a desire to shield him from the harsh truth, a testament to their complex bond. Had Jerrie been aware of Gianna's insecurity, would it have been beneficial for the well-being of their relationship to share it with Issac, potentially leading to the preservation of their marriage?

However, the investigators were not swayed by the explanation provided by Jerrie. A cloud of doubt hung over Jerrie's role, with allegations of manipulation and ulterior motives. He capitalized on Gianna's fragile mental state, employing the saved letters as a cloak to obscure a more sinister truth—a truth that pointed to murder rather than suicide.

The story unfolded against a backdrop of contrasting personalities. Issac, a reserved individual who shied away from confrontation, and Jerrie, a charismatic presence who seemed to exert a significant influence over him. As suspicions rise, the dynamics of their relationship come under scrutiny, with questions swirling about who truly held the reins.

As the case unfolded, the journey through court and investigation began to take center stage. A diverse array of opinions emerged, each with its interpretation of the evidence. The debate raged on— Did Gianna take her own life, or was her death a consequence of malevolent actions?

In the end, as the trial wrapped up, the jury found itself at an impasse, unable to definitively pronounce judgment. The ambiguity persisted, leaving Gianna's death cloaked in a shroud of uncertainty. The truth remained elusive, obscured by the intricate interplay of emotions, relationships, and circumstances beyond any comprehension.

Suicide was not ruled out in the case because of these and other letters that were presented later in the trial and could prove this was a very real possibility.

In these letters, Gianna also demonstrates thoughtfulness toward Jerrie, suggesting that his decision to extend his stay might have stemmed from concerns about their well-being and the return journey to Toronto alongside Issac.

Chapter 6

It seemed to be an intricate web of speculation, where secrets and shadows intertwined, painting a cryptic picture of a fateful honeymoon turned into tragedy. In the heart of this enigma were three individuals—Gianna, Issac, and Jerrie—each linked by threads of love, intrigue, and suspicion. It revealed a story that seemed to be haunted by the possibility of truth slipping through the fingers.

The first theory to emerge was one of insurance fraud—a plot hatched by John and Jerrie, casting the dark shadow of greed and deceit over their once idyllic honeymoon. The focus shifts to Jerrie's cottage, which was insured with John as the beneficiary, raising eyebrows at the convenient timing. Further investigation began to reveal that John had entrusted his war gratuity to Jerrie, blurring the line between friendship and financial ties.

The puzzle grew more intriguing as life insurance policies came into play. John takes out $5,000 policies on both himself and Gianna, but the real twist lies in the fine print—double the payout in case of accidental death. Jerrie, with a background in insurance and construction, becomes a key figure, fuelling suspicions that extend beyond financial motives. A veil of ambiguity surrounds the nature of John and Jerrie's relationship, adding yet another layer to the conspiracy theory.

As the case dived deeper, a second theory emerged, casting a spotlight on Gianna's struggles. Mental illness took center stage, intertwining with the shadowy threads of her life. The inquest didn't just unravel scandalous details about the men; it uncovered disconcerting facts about Gianna's inner turmoil. The theory posits that she was tormented by a mental illness that ultimately led her down a tragic path, possibly even driving her to attempt her husband's life.

Gianna's alleged mental state was reflected in a series of alarming letters written in the months preceding her death. The letters, a vivid testimony to her pain, become a haunting puzzle piece. Penned in moments of darkness, they speak of her despair, her desire to escape a world that seemed too cruel to bear. The words etched on paper reveal a woman wrestling with her demons, her mind gripped by the shadows. These letters trace a chilling timeline, beginning five weeks before her wedding. During that period, their engagement had not yet taken place.

Jerrie's role takes on a new dimension as he emerges as the recipient of many of these letters. His knowledge of Gianna's fragile state casts a pall over his involvement in their lives. Could his presence on their honeymoon have been an attempt to avert tragedy, to shield Gianna from herself? One letter, addressed to the owner of their Toronto apartment, hints at the finality of her decision, evoking a sense of impending doom.

Jerrie's claims of lending her money deepen the intrigue, as financial strain joins the fray. Gianna held a modestly paid position at a bank, making it challenging for her to reimburse the substantial sum of money. Jerrie expressed that he didn't anticipate repayment, considering the money a gesture of friendship. During his testimony, he claimed that she had returned $12,000 to him. He also stated that he entrusted her with money to deposit in his bank account, but the funds were never credited back to his account.

The climax comes in Gianna's final letter—a plea for help and an acknowledgment of the turmoil within her. It becomes Jerrie's mission to preserve these letters, saving them from the flames that consume their cabin. As the trial unfolds, these letters stand as a testament to the turmoil that gripped Gianna's soul. Maybe Jerrie utilized these letters effectively to support his defense.

Yet another theory loomed—a sinister partnership between Issac and Jerrie, working together to orchestrate Gianna's demise. Issac's life insurance policy on Gianna raised eyebrows, promising him a payout upon her death. The duo's history of questionable insurance dealings fuelled speculation, tainting their motives with shades of manipulation and greed.

As the investigation continued, one undeniable fact persisted—the close bond between Issac and Jerrie. This revelation added complexity to their dynamics.

The tale took a morbid turn as the media capitalized on the sensational aspect of the case, casting Issac as a tragic heartthrob in the public eye. He starts indulging in his newfound fame, even signing autographs for those who recognized him from the headlines. Amidst the chaos, the truth remained elusive, obscured by a veil of unanswered questions.

In the end, the theories collided, each with its narrative, evidence, and ambiguity. Neither of the men get arrested, and they were seen as victims of the fire. They become celebrities overnight. There were no indications of remorse regarding Gianna's passing, raising doubts about the veracity of Gianna's claim that her affection for Jerrie was unrequited and one-sided. In the spotlight were Issac and Jerrie - the crowds swarmed around them as if their very presence held the key to solving the enigmatic puzzle that was Gianna's death.

Chapter 7

The official verdict, a ruling of drowning, resonated with the eerie stillness of a calm river surface. Yet, beneath this tranquil facade, a storm of complexity brewed, for toxicology reports presented a discordant note. Traces of codeine, a substance that begged further exploration, were discovered in Gianna's stomach. This revelation cast doubt on the simplicity of the narrative, injecting an element of uncertainty into the prevailing understanding of events.

Major Daniel Gutierrez, a witness to the unfolding tragedy, added an intriguing dimension. His account of battling the flames while Jerrie accompanied Issac to the hospital bore an unexpected twist – he had not seen Gianna's lifeless form near the water source, despite his actions coinciding with the location where her body would later be discovered. This unsettling detail transformed a straightforward firefighting effort into an enigma that defied explanation.

The absence of marks on Gianna's bare feet further fuelled speculation. How could she have walked to the river's edge from the cabin without leaving a trace? It was a perplexing puzzle piece, hinting at a narrative that may have been manipulated or obscured.

The absence of burn marks and any indicators of violence on Gianna's body was a stark contrast to the events that transpired on that fateful day. How could a fire have raged, consuming her surroundings, while leaving her untouched? The unsettling possibility emerged – had she been placed in the river after the fire's extinguishment, her death shrouded in a veil of calculated deception?

The narrative twisted yet again with the revelation of Issac's confession, laying bare a long-term affair with Jerrie. However, this confession's authenticity waned as Issac later claimed coercion by authorities. The shifting sands of truth and manipulation blurred the lines of reality, leaving behind a lingering question – was this confession a genuine revelation or a pawn in a more intricate scheme?

Jerrie's admission of experimentation with Issac, driven by curiosity, contrasted sharply with his assertion that nothing had occurred between them since 1939. This revelation added layers to the evolving storyline, casting Jerrie in an enigmatic light that begged further exploration.

The watchful eyes of Celestial Falls locals bore witness to Issac and Jerrie's frequent cottage trips, raising eyebrows and prompting whispers of curiosity. These escapades cast an aura of peculiarity around the two men, painting them as enigmas in the eyes of their community.

Tucked within the folds of Gianna's letters was evidence of her discomfort with the intimacy shared between Issac and Jerrie. These correspondences formed a trail of emotional breadcrumbs, hinting at a web of complex relationships that extended far beyond the surface.

The twist in the tale emerged as Jerrie safeguarded Gianna's letters from the fire's ravages. The act, while appearing protective on the surface, ignited suspicions that he may have capitalized on her fragile mental state, turning her vulnerability into a weapon that concealed a sinister truth.

The murky waters of the drug trafficking angle added yet another layer of intrigue. Gianna appeared to be under the influence of drugs. A luxury apartment in Toronto, rumored to serve as the headquarters of this operation, added a touch of sophistication to an otherwise rustic narrative. The juxtaposition of glamour against the backdrop of Gianna's death underscored the multifaceted nature of the unfolding tale.

The mystery surrounding Gianna's ring further complicated matters. The conflicting reports, each attributing its purchase to different characters, deepened the enigma. Mrs. Lukas's claim, stating the ring was hers and loaned for the wedding ceremony, left an unresolved riddle in the wake of Gianna's passing.

Celine's belief that Gianna had been drugged before her marriage revealed a dark undercurrent. The suggestion that she accepted her fate out of fear for both men painted a chilling picture of psychological manipulation, intertwining fear, and uncertainty with her tragic end.

Mrs. Lukas's apprehensions about Jerrie's honeymoon plans served as an eerie premonition, hinting at a foreboding that loomed over the narrative. Her perception of Issac as Jerrie's assistant and her characterization of Jerrie as a manipulator added depth to something that sounded more like a manipulation.

Jerrie's financial complications confounded authorities, sparking questions about his money transactions.

Jerrie's testimony of Gianna's request for financial assistance following a church attack in 1946, added a new dimension to the case. The extortion and threat she faced introduced a grim underbelly, a subplot that painted a darker hue on the canvas of Gianna's life.

The loan of $12,000 from Jerrie to Gianna, and his explanation of doing it out of friendship, left authorities perplexed. The incongruity between his generous loan and her meager earnings cast a shadow over his intentions, leaving questions lingering in the air.

Chapter 8

There seemed to be a puzzling juxtaposition between the assertion that events would conclude and the act of mailing the letter itself raised a myriad of questions. How could Gianna anticipate the conclusion of events while simultaneously tasking Jerrie with delivering this letter? Was it possible that she had intended to send this message before Jerrie's return, hinting at a narrative yet untold? Or did she approach Mrs. Lukas for assistance, realizing that her time was running out and seeking a way to be saved?

The complexities deepened as the events of that pivotal day came into focus. Jerrie was embarking on sunbathing, an action that seemed to align with Gianna's note. Yet, the act of mailing the letter seemed incongruous with the notion of impending resolution. Perhaps, as suggested, Gianna had intended to convey her thoughts to Mrs. Lukas before the anticipated events would unfold.

Jerrie's return was meant to herald the conclusion of the saga. The implication that "Jerrie is in the boat outside somewhere" cast a shadow of premonition, suggesting that Gianna was aware of impending developments. The statement that "everything will be all over with" upon his return hinted at a profound event horizon, a turning point in her narrative.

Yet, the discrepancy between the anticipated conclusion and the act of mailing the letter prompted a cascade of speculation. Did Gianna plan to end her own life or orchestrate a murder-suicide with Jerrie?

Issac and Jerrie, bound by a longstanding friendship and business partnership, shared an intimacy that extended beyond societal norms. Their relationship, characterized by occasional sexual interactions, hinted at a depth of connection that transcended convention.

The astonishing narrative revolved around her being assaulted by multiple men during a church dance, and these men were using blackmail as leverage. They threatened to reveal the incident to her parents unless she complied with their demands for payment.

Gianna's tragic narrative was interwoven with a disturbing account of assault and blackmail. The dark shadow cast by her alleged violation and subsequent threats painted a poignant backdrop for her turmoil. The cloud of blackmail loomed, forcing her into a web of vulnerability and fear, the weight of which would become inextricably entwined with her choices.

Her sister's assertions of Gianna's fear of both men added yet another layer to the complexity of her character. Gianna was drugged before her marriage. This latest development in the case cast a shadow of doubt over the authenticity of her relationship with Issac.

The chain of events leading to Gianna's death provided an unsettling tableau. Jerrie's account of that pivotal day revealed a series of actions that defied easy explanation. Gianna's apparent calmness, Issac's sudden unconsciousness, and the head wound Jerrie described presented a perplexing puzzle. The letter she had entrusted to Jerrie hinted at an impending resolution, while the fire that consumed the cabin told a tale of its own.

The trail of uncertainty led to speculation about Issac's involvement and his subsequent amnesia. Gianna's feet, undamaged despite her supposed trek through bushes, raised questions about the sequence of events and the possibility of her being carried to her final resting place.

Indeed, it appeared that Jerrie was the orchestrator of the entire narrative. He operated a dual role, seemingly a friend to Gianna, yet manipulating her by administering drugs and coercing her to write distressing letters while she was mentally unwell. Jerrie sowed seeds of doubt in Gianna's mind regarding Isaac's affections, while simultaneously safeguarding his close friend, Isaac, and concocting a plan to eliminate Gianna to gain financial benefits from insurance policies.

Isaac and Jerrie had a longstanding companionship, both as business partners and roommates, and they acknowledged having engaged in a romantic relationship at some point. Their sexual orientation extended to being bisexual. It is plausible that Jerrie harbored desires for Isaac exclusively and was unwilling to share him with Gianna, potentially motivating his actions.

Issac agreed to be playing a part by agreeing to be drugged and struck over the head and hoping that the damage wasn't too bad.

It did seem like a perfect storm scenario - Jerrie is not doing well with his business ventures and wants money. Issac is an easily manipulated person who wants to live with Jerrie in peace without any stress or pressure. Gianna is suicidal and desperate to "normalize" her life. Jerrie - already being acquainted with these people - sees all this as a perfect opportunity to give everyone want, they want.

At some point, Gianna was forced to write that last suicide letter, which would not seem suspicious due to her history. On the final day, Gianna was drugged, brought down to the river, and Jerrie drowned her. Jerrie had already gathered up everything important in the cabin and had set it on fire.

Chapter 9

In the annals of crime, the allure of financial gain often emerges as a central motive. The underlying thread in Gianna's demise seemed to be a scheme of insurance fraud. Jerrie had insured his cottage for a substantial sum and designated Issac as the beneficiary. Further complicating matters, Issac had taken out life insurance policies, valuing 500 Canadian dollars each, on both himself and Gianna. What is more, Jerrie stood as the beneficiary of these policies.

The intricate web of insurance policies thickened with a significant clause: if the deaths were deemed accidental, the payout amount would be doubled. The potential financial windfall created a striking incentive that cast a shadow of suspicion over the events that unfolded.

Gianna's missing wedding ring became a focal point of contention, further intensifying the intrigue. The value of the ring and its whereabouts remained unknown.

The case's complexity deepened with the potential implication of a romantic relationship between the men. Their emotional connection, coupled with financial motivations, became a compelling case for foul play.

Gianna, the unfortunate bride who had passed away, was portrayed as a vulnerable woman, unable to defend herself even in death. She was depicted as a woman besieged by overwhelming emotions and a consuming infatuation for Issac. The emergence of multiple suicide letters, composed in the period leading up to her passing, illuminated the stormy nature of her mental well-being. Within these letters, a range of emotions was conveyed, spanning from desolation to a troubling yearning for a shared demise.

Jerrie, to assert that Gianna had taken her own life and to divert attention from the calculated scheme involving the two men, managed to rescue all of the letters from a cabin fire. These letters were subsequently presented in court, serving to bolster his position. The aim was seemingly to cast a shadow over the brewing scandal and refocus the narrative away from the intricate plans of the two men.

Jerrie entered the cabin and discovered Gianna, who appeared disoriented and had tears streaming down her cheeks. Issac lay unconscious nearby. Recognizing an opportunity, Jerrie initiated a fire within his cottage, seemingly to file an insurance claim for accidental fire. He proceeded to carry Issac to safety outside the cabin.

Returning for Gianna, he carried her towards the water, possibly aiming to rouse her from a drugged state. However, a sudden realization struck him – a macabre notion of utilizing Gianna's demise to secure insurance funds. In her semi-conscious state, he left her unattended, allowing her to succumb. This clarifies why she hadn't been discovered by the water earlier, as she remained inside the cottage.

Chapter 10

Within the depths of this tragic tale, two men emerge from the shadows—Issac and Jerrie—bearing their enigmas and secrets. The tendrils of suspicion wind around them, hinting at a sinister partnership or an insidious plot. The evidence paints a vivid picture of deception, woven through the fabric of insurance policies and financial transactions.

Issac's decision to procure life insurance policies veiled in suspicion, along with Jerrie's labyrinthine connections, cast an eerie shadow over their innocence. The double indemnity clauses, the mysterious policies, and Jerrie's checkered career in construction and insurance form a tapestry of intrigue that refuses to be ignored.

Issac had initially asserted that he and Jerrie had shared an intimate relationship for a period. However, during the court proceedings, Issac contended that he had been coerced into making that statement by the police, who sought to construct that narrative in their report. Indeed, the police commissioner's report on Gianna's case touched upon this relationship, characterizing it as "unconventional," if not unnatural. While evidence was lacking to substantiate this claim, suspicions remained high.

During the inquest, Crown Counsel C.P. Hope challenged Issac's assertion of coercion and proposed that the two were indeed romantically involved. After persistent questioning from Hope, Issac eventually acceded to this assertion. Under rigorous cross-examination, Issac and Jerrie were involved as male partners, and the intricate web of tangled and suppressed emotions began to take shape.

Although the direct cause of her death wasn't directly attributed to the two men, they were aware of her intentions and capitalized on her vulnerable state. Jerrie potentially shared the letters with Issac, possibly even encouraging Gianna's fragile mental state and her anxieties about Issac's feelings. Recognizing that she was contemplating a drastic step, they procured insurance policies and ensured Jerrie was present as a precaution in case her plans took a violent turn. This could explain Jerrie's preservation of the letters, salvaging them from the fire, to demonstrate her state of mind and affirm their innocence.

Gianna had paranoid tendencies, so when she either found out or assumed the relationship between Issac and Jerrie she snapped. She took drugs, drugged Issac, and tried to murder him by knocking him out. Jerrie showed up just in time to save Issac.

Chapter 11

Issac and Jerrie weren't facing a murder trial. Rather, the case aimed to establish whether Gianna's demise involved any foul play. Amidst the extensively sensationalized investigation, various intriguing details emerged. Eventually, the inquest jury concurred that Gianna's death was indeed a result of foul play, leading to a clear verdict of guilt for Issac and Jerrie. The trial unveiled their connections to both Gianna and each other, laying bare their intricate relationships.

Signs and evidence indicated that Gianna was deeply troubled by the "unconventional behavior of her spouse and Jerrie."

The coincidence of both becoming engrossed in insurance matters was certainly peculiar.

Issac and Jerrie were in a relationship but Issac obligatorily married Gianna to avoid persecution. A romantic involvement between two men appeared to be a social taboo. They burned down the cottage on purpose to claim insurance and were expecting Gianna to poison herself. The men probably knew of her suicidal ideation which is why they saved the letters so there weren't any murder accusations.

Recovered items don't always surface after being pawned; they dismantled the wedding ring to melt down its gold. It had been sold to jewelers for use in custom jewelry, rendering identification of specific pieces challenging after a complete disassembly. As a result, they successfully cashed in by selling the ring and evaded detection.

Jerrie and Issac were involved in a romantic relationship. Locals near Jerrie's cabin frequently observed the two visiting alone, a behavior that struck them as peculiar. During their police statements, some officers noted that the connection between the two seemed "unusual." Despite a lack of concrete evidence validating their relationship, letters penned by Gianna before her death hinted at her discomfort with the "unnatural" closeness between the men.

Ultimately, justice prevailed, leading to the incarceration of both men, Issac and Jerrie, for life. This served as a modest yet fitting tribute to Gianna's premature passing for her family.

About the Author

D.S. Pais

D.S. Pais, a globally celebrated and bestselling author, possesses an innate gift for envisioning new worlds. From her early years, she's been captivated by a boundless imagination, nurturing her passion for writing. While she initially explored her creativity through acting in student films and television series, her true calling emerged when she discovered the magic of storytelling through writing.

Her artistic range spans diverse forms including short stories, novellas, novels, poetry, and self-help books, as writing remains the only vessel vast enough to encapsulate her myriad thoughts.

Beyond the realm of literature, D.S. Pais finds solace in the pages of books, the allure of movies, the thrill of travel, and the rejuvenation of Pilates and other exercises.

With an ardent dedication to her craft, D.S. Pais actively engages with multiple book projects annually, all underscored by her fervent commitment to the art of narrative. Her creations frequently ascend to the upper echelons of success, often gracing the Amazon Best Sellers list across various genres.

While her roots trace back to India, D.S. Pais now proudly embraces Singaporean citizenship, residing in the vibrant city-state with her husband and two cherished children.

For more insights into her world, you can explore D.S. Pais's YouTube channel at,

https://www.youtube.com/channel/UC3k5wx5eX2_al M0joxJxk5g?sub_confirmation=1

www.ingramcontent.com/pod-product-compliance
Lightning Source LLC
LaVergne TN
LVHW041554070526
838199LV00046B/1957